BOOK 9

JENNA AND THE
BROKEN PROMISE

THE ITURIA CHRONICLES

J.B. MOONSTAR

BOOK 9

JENNA AND THE BROKEN PROMISE

THE ITURIA CHRONICLES

J.B. MOONSTAR

Jenna and the Broken Promise
Copyright © 2022 J.B. Moonstar. All rights reserved.

Published By: The Little Horsemen an imprint of 4 Horsemen Publications, Inc.

The Little Horsemen Publications
℅ 4 Horsemen Publications, Inc.
PO Box 419
Sylva, NC 28779
4horsemenpublications.com
info@4horsemenpublications.com

Cover &Illustration by Jenn Kotick. Contact for commssions at Jkotickart@gmail.com .

Typesetting by Michelle Cline

Editor CI Stearns

Library of Congress Control Number: 2022931354

Paperback ISBN-13: 978-1-64450-542-7
Hardcover ISBN-13: 978-1-64450-655-4
Audiobook ISBN-13: 978-1-64450-536-6
Ebook ISBN-13: 978-1-64450-537-3

DEDICATION

Dedicated to all those who work to
protect wild animals and their habitats.
Thank you!

Dear Reader,

After Jenna used Ituria's magic to turn hunter Ike into a tree to keep him from hurting her grandpa and Ralphie, things started returning to normal—at least for a few months. Now, one of the hunters who came with Ike to find a dragon has returned, and he's asking a lot of questions. This hunter, Mitch, also claims to have seen a dragon, and he is suspicious of Jenna because of Ike's story that he saw her turn into a wolf.

Realizing that he can no longer use Middle Forest as a base, Ituria has asked the Elders to consider appointing Jenna as its newest Protector. Jenna must make a decision that will affect not only her life, but the life of all the inhabitants of Ituria's home base on Earth.

But first she must deal with the threat of Mitch in Middle Forest. Will she be able to outsmart Mitch, or will he succeed where Ike failed? And how will she, a 12-year-old human, appear to the Elders—will they consider her worthy to serve as the first human Protector?

Join me as we learn how Jenna deals with this newest threat to Ituria's Alliance, and if she has the courage and spirit to take on the role of Protector of Middle Forest!

Sincerely,

Knocker,

First Guard to Ituria

TABLE OF CONTENTS

Chapter One

SECRETS REVEALED

Jenna looked out from the back yard into the forest beyond. Her memories of transforming into a wolf to protect her grandpa and her fox friend Ralphie seemed far away, almost unreal. Looking at her grandfather resting in the chair next to her, the setting sun gave him the shadow of a bear, and now she understood why.

Over the past few months, her grandpa told her several stories of his adventures with Knocker and Ituria. He told her how he met Ituria and Knocker many, many years ago when he was just a boy. She smiled as she remembered the first adventure grandpa shared, his earliest trip to the moon to visit Ituria's Islands, and how he helped solve a mystery that was killing the plants in the caverns of the moon, threatening the lives of all the inhabitants.

Jenna was fascinated to learn that Ituria, a majestic white unicorn, modified a series of caverns on the moon so they could provide homes to animals that were being needlessly killed by humans on

Earth. Grandpa also told her of his role in Ituria's Alliance, a secret organization on Earth, composed of both humans and animals, to help Ituria on his rescue missions.

Knocker, a large dragon assigned as Ituria's First Guard, joined them on several occasions for their evening talks near the forest's edge. His translation stone allowed Jenna and her grandfather to understand his dragon speak, and he stayed in the shadows of the forest so he would not be seen by anyone else during their meetings.

Knocker revealed to Jenna there was a magic potion that allowed him to transform into a human for a short period of time, if needed, while on rescue missions. Using the potion and having a translation stone allowed him to blend in with humans while on Earth. He also shared some of his recent adventures, including one where his mission was to rescue endangered tern chicks, and noted Jenna's grandpa was part of his tern rescue team. While talking with Jenna and Grandpa, Knocker saw Ituria heading their way through the forest.

"Knocker," Ituria called out in a worried voice as he got closer. "We have an issue that needs to be resolved. Please review the most recent recording sent by Dan's seal. Russ and Jenna, please watch also, as it concerns Ike."

Jenna gave Grandpa a worried look as they walked toward Ituria. *What is going on—how can Ike be involved? I turned him into a tree in Middle Forest!*

Ituria nodded his head and a large gourd appeared on the table in the back yard near the edge of the forest. A small oval screen was visible on the bottom half of the gourd, looking like a small television screen. They watched silently as the video started playing.

The screen revealed a room; the camera was facing one of the walls. Wooden planks lined the wall, and a hammer and other tools were visible on a table. A man's forearm was visible on the screen, picking up and turning something around, then putting it down again. A phone rang and a hand picked it up, pushed a button, then put the phone back on the table.

"Hello, this is Dan," said a voice in a businesslike manner. The screen moved up and down a bit, as if the camera holder was working on something.

"Hey, Dan, this is Mitch, how are you doing?" Mitch said in a friendly manner.

"I'm okay. Do I know you?" Dan replied, a little concerned.

"Well, we may not have met, but one of my friends told me that you had a hunting business, but then sold it about a year or so ago. Is that correct?" Mitch asked.

"Yep, sold it all, got another job," Dan answered. "I'm at work now. What's up?"

"Well, I just wanted to make sure I have the right Dan," Mitch said with a chuckle. "So, I hear you had a hunting job in North Carolina just before you sold the business. Is that right?"

"Yeah, so what?" Dan said, his voice getting defensive, the camera stopped moving, and so did the forearm.

"Well, when my friend called you about the job, he said you didn't want to talk about it, and if he was in the area, you told him to just leave and don't look back. Is that right?" Mitch asked, his voice indicating that he hoped that wasn't what really happened.

"Look, I'll tell you the same thing I told your friend. Leave that area alone!" Dan said, almost shouting.

"But why?" Mitch asked. "I really need to know."

"I'm not going to discuss it, okay? It's none of your business!" Dan said. "Now if you continue to ask about that job, I'm just going to hang up."

"Well, I was wondering if you would join me on a little hunting trip, totally different area. Could you do that?" Mitch was trying to be friendly, but he was insistent.

"I don't go hunting anymore," Dan replied, very irritated, and a hand was seen moving toward the phone, picking it up again.

"Okay, we won't go hunting. I just want to explore an area where I was a few months ago. I'm looking for someone and maybe you can help me find him. He disappeared and I haven't been able to reach him since. Do you know an Ike Monnihan?" Mitch asked, continuing with his questions.

"Nope, never heard of him. No hunting, right?" Dan insisted. "I will not go hunting again!"

"I'm looking for someone, so it's kind of a rescue mission you could say. I want to find out what happened to him. No hunting!" Mitch agreed with a chuckle.

"Does it pay?" Dan asked. He wasn't going anywhere without a fee.

"Yes, you bet. I'll pay top dollar to find Ike. I'll send you the paperwork!" Mitch said, excited he had at least gotten Dan to meet him and look for Ike.

"Okay, send me the paperwork, and I'll let you know when I'm available," Dan replied, his voice calmer now.

"It needs to be as soon as possible, okay?" Mitch answered.

"Okay, send the check. I'll deposit it. If it's enough and if the check clears, then we can meet whenever you want," Dan said. "Got to get back to work now. Bye."

The screen went blank. Ituria looked up at Knocker and in a concerned voice said, "A hunter named Mitch is heading to Middle Forest and says he is looking for Ike."

Chapter Two

NO LONGER SAFE

"Ituria," Knocker began. "I recognize Mitch's voice. He was the hunter Megan was up against on the rescue of the last nine red wolves from North Carolina about a month ago. Mitch saw Megan as a dragon. I approached Mitch in human form after the final nine red wolves were transported to the moon, and I asked him to promise never to hunt again. Mitch gave me his promise he would never hunt again."

"Ituria," Jenna said, adding her information to Knocker's report, "Grandpa and I have seen Mitch also; he was a member of Ike's hunting party a few months ago. Ike told Mitch about seeing Knocker in Middle Forest right after he shot Ranco and Trent. He also told Mitch about me turning into a wolf and attacking him."

Glancing at Grandpa as she spoke, Jenna added, "We managed to convince Mitch otherwise at the time, but if he has now seen a dragon, he may be on his way back to Middle Forest to continue Ike's quest."

"I was afraid this would happen," Ituria said in a frustrated voice. "One hunter will spread tales, and there will always be other hunters to follow. Dan said he would never hunt again, and I believe him because he has my seal always watching him. So, Mitch is going to call it a 'rescue mission.' However, I doubt that is what Mitch really has in mind."

"What are your orders, Ituria?" Knocker asked solemnly.

"Knocker, you must not be in dragon form in Middle Forest," Ituria responded. "That is my first concern, that he will find you. If Mitch breaks his promise to you and attempts to hunt here, he cannot find you as a dragon."

"Russ," Ituria continued, "if Mitch is indeed heading back this way, we may need to enlist your help as well as Jenna's."

"We will be glad to help. Just let us know what is needed!" Grandpa replied immediately, then added, "I would like to know what the plans are, though, and how Jenna will be involved, as my first concern is to make sure she is safe."

"Understood," Ituria agreed and nodded. "Jenna, your courage and spirit were inspiring as you protected your grandfather and my friends. We may need you to assist us once again if Mitch shows up here."

"I will be glad to help protect my animal friends," Jenna replied at once, ready for whatever Ituria asked her to do to.

"Thank you, Jenna," Ituria replied. "Knocker, your first two assignments are to transport Celeste up to our moon home, and then to find Simon to give you the transformation potion so you can use it here to be ready for Mitch."

"Yes, Ituria," Knocker said, accepting his assignments. "I will proceed immediately!" Knocker was turning from the group to start his first mission when Ituria called him back.

"Knocker, one moment. I need to tell you something." Ituria paused for a moment and then continued with sadness. "With these recent events, I have decided that Middle Forest can no longer be our base when we come to Earth. There is too much danger for you as well as to myself and my family. I will need to talk to the Elders on how they want to protect Middle Forest once we leave. It is important that a Protector is assigned to keep this region and its residents safe."

"I agree, Ituria," Knocker responded with concern. "It is no longer safe for you and Celeste to visit here, and you should not return. I will do whatever the Elders require once you have consulted with them."

"Thank you, Knocker," Ituria continued in a serious tone. "While I am visiting the Elders, will you take the transformation medicine and stay with Russ and Jenna, to protect them should Mitch show up? I will be back within the week that the transformation potion works. That would be my request once you have taken Celeste to safety."

"Of course, Ituria," Knocker replied with resolve. "It will be my honor!"

Chapter Three

MITCH PAYS A VISIT

Plans were made between Grandpa and Jenna's parents to allow Knocker to spend the week at their house. Grandpa explained an old friend of his had a grandson that needed to spend the week while the friend was traveling, and Jenna's mom and dad agreed to allow Knocker to stay.

While Grandpa was making the final arrangements, Knocker, now in his human form, and Jenna, were sitting under a tree in the woods near her house, talking. As a human, Knocker appeared as a teenage boy about fourteen years old with shoulder length black hair wearing a tee shirt and jeans; he was carrying a duffle bag over his shoulder.

Ralphie, a fox friend of Jenna's, saw them under the tree and came over to visit, and since Knocker had his translation stone in his bag, Ralphie could join in their conversation.

As Ralphie walked over and sat next to her, Jenna said to him, "Ralphie, I'm so glad to see you! Knocker is going to come to our house for a few days. One of the hunters who was here a few months ago is back, and we need to be ready. I don't know if you will be safe in the woods, and I was hoping you would stay with us also. Do you think you could do that?"

"They're back?" Ralphie said, his voice trembling with fear. "I remember being caught in their trap; I don't want to be out in the woods when they are here. Yes, please, may I stay with you and Knocker?"

Putting her arm around Ralphie and giving him a warm hug, Jenna replied softly, "Ralphie, I don't want you to have to go through that ever again. You are welcome at my house whenever you want, and you can stay as long as you want. Please remember that!"

Ralphie nodded at Jenna and rested his head on her knee; she gently stroked his back as she turned to continue her conversation with Knocker. Ralphie relaxed and closed his eyes, knowing Jenna would keep him safe.

"Knocker," Jenna started, "do you think we need to let the other animals know about…?" then stopped as she heard footsteps in the distance. Looking in the direction of the sound, she saw Mitch heading their way. It had only been three days since Mitch called Dan, and Mitch's "rescue mission" was moving ahead fast. Jenna put her arm around Ralphie and gently pulled him closer to her. "Remember, no talking, Ralphie, okay?" she whispered.

Knocker and Jenna watched silently as Mitch approached them, waiting for him to speak first.

"So, little lady, it's been a while, hasn't it?" he started in a friendly tone. "I haven't been able to find Ike yet, and I wanted to know if he ever came back here, and also, I wanted to find out why Ike was so upset when you and he met in the forest a few months ago."

Jenna looked up at Mitch for a few moments, thinking about how to respond, then answered calmly. "Mitch, isn't it? Don't you remember what happened? Ike wanted to take my fox, and it bit him."

She gently stroked Ralphie's back as he lifted his head, looking at her anxiously. "We ran away, and he followed. You and the others were able to keep him from coming back to my house. Thank you for keeping him away from my Ralphie." Jenna hoped this would work but wasn't sure. Mitch moved closer, looming over her and Ralphie.

"Hi, I'm Marcus," said Knocker, trying to draw Mitch's attention away from Jenna. "I wasn't here when you met Jenna last time. What happened?"

"Oh … don't I know you? You look very familiar to me," replied Mitch suspiciously, looking at Knocker closely.

"No, I don't think so," Knocker replied without any emotion. "Are you from around here?"

"Do you know someone named Knocker? You look close enough alike to be related," Mitch said, still looking at Knocker.

"Knocker?" Knocker said calmly. "That's an interesting name. Doesn't sound familiar. Where did you meet this Knocker person?"

"Oh, never mind. It was night when I met him, so maybe I didn't get a good look," Mitch said, turning to focus on Jenna and Ralphie again.

11

"Marcus, this is Mitch. He was here a few months ago," Jenna said to introduce them. "Mitch was here with Ike, and Ike claimed he had seen a dragon in the area and was back to catch it—kill it and cut off its head—just to prove that he had seen a dragon!" Jenna's voice was stressed as she continued, "And Mitch was here to help him kill the dragon."

"Okay, let me explain," Mitch said lightheartedly, trying to erase the ominous tone Jenna used. "This is what really happened; it was something. My old friend Ike told me that he had seen a dragon here in the forest. So, he dragged me and three other guys out here to find it. The only thing I saw was a fox that he caught in a trap. Then this little lady shows up and claims the fox is hers."

Mitch paused and looked at Jenna, waiting for her to speak. Jenna just stared at Mitch and continued petting Ralphie, trying to keep him calm. She could feel him shaking as he remembered the terrible day he was caught in the Ike's trap.

"Well," Mitch continued, "an argument ensued, and Ike refused to let her have her pet." Mitch puffed his chest out and proudly said, "I stepped in and told her she could have it, and let her leave, right little girl? I let you keep your pet there!"

Jenna nodded slowly a few times, remembering it wasn't Mitch who let her leave with Ralphie, but Bob. Mitch was too busy taunting Ike about the dragon he claimed to have seen.

Mitch paused again, wanting Jenna to add something to his story. Looking directly at Jenna, he started again in a rougher tone, "After Ike realized she was gone and had taken the fox, he ran after her. About twenty minutes later, he ran back here screaming that this little lady had turned into a wolf and had attacked him. He showed us his hand; it had very large teeth marks and gashes. Does *that* sound familiar?"

"I remember him saying something like that when he came by my house," Jenna calmly replied. "But it didn't make sense at the time. He pulled a knife on me and tried to grab my fox. Ralphie bit him on the hand rather badly, twisting and turning while biting him. Then Ike ran away."

Mitch got closer, leaning over Jenna again and pointing his finger at her. "That's not what he said, little lady, but we will have to take your word for it … for now."

Ralphie was terrified now, he hid his head under his tail as he curled into a ball next to Jenna.

Knocker scooted closer to Jenna, so he was sitting next to her and Ralphie, able to react if Mitch tried to do anything more than talk. Mitch noticed and started talking directly to Knocker to plead his case.

"Oh, yeah, she made it home with her little fox, made it home to her grandpa," Mitch told Knocker. "We convinced the grandpa not to call the cops and I took Ike back to my camp."

"Well," Knocker replied, "looks like Jenna got her fox back, so it all ended well."

"No, it didn't," said Mitch with a little smirk, "at least not for Ike."

Chapter Four

WHAT HAPPENED TO IKE?

Jenna looked up at Mitch, wondering what he might know, and asked, "Why? What happened to him?"

"Well," Mitch continued, talking quickly now, "he slipped us some sort of sleeping pills and got out of camp. We didn't wake until almost morning, and he was gone. We came to your house first, but Ike wasn't there. You and your grandpa were on the porch with your foxie. Then we searched the woods. The only thing we found was his knife, thrown into a campfire. That was something Ike wouldn't have done … and we haven't heard from him since." Mitch's story stopped as he stared at Jenna, waiting for her to add something more to complete the story.

"Maybe he just ran away, since he had made such a fool of himself," Jenna suggested.

"You know," Mitch replied, eyeing Jenna and Ralphie, "that's what we thought too. But he never made it home, hasn't been to his house since, and it's been a few months now. I've been asking around and calling his friends, but no one seems to know where he is."

"Were you close friends?" Knocker asked. "Maybe you could check with his family. They might have some information on him."

"Oh, I checked, but they hadn't seen him," Mitch replied. "Since we weren't the best of friends, the family wasn't too keen to share anything with me…"

"So maybe he did go home," Jenna interjected, "and just told his family they were not to talk to you if you came around."

Mitch looked at Jenna closely. "Or…" he said slowly, "maybe he never left the forest."

"Do you think he is still here, maybe hiding out or something?" Jenna asked anxiously, pulling Ralphie even closer; he was still shaking with fear.

"Well, I'm not sure. His knife was found in a campfire, and he would never have thrown it there… why would he still be here?" Mitch asked suspiciously. "And if he is still here, where do you think he would be?"

Again, Mitch was watching Jenna closely, waiting for her to give him some clue, some explanation, for Ike's disappearance.

"I hope he's not still here," she replied. "But if you say he hasn't turned up, I need to let my grandpa know. Ike and Grandpa don't get along and I'm afraid Ike might do something bad to Grandpa. Maybe we should call the police and report him as missing—have you done that yet?"

Mitch replied quickly, "Now don't go jumping to conclusions, young lady. I was just wondering what you might know."

Knocker joined in the conversation again, wanting to draw out Mitch's side of the story. "So, you have reported him as missing, right?"

That stopped Mitch's rambling, and for once he didn't know what to say.

After a few seconds waiting for Mitch to answer, Knocker continued in a serious tone. "Do you think he is really missing—or possibly is he just avoiding you and any others who might have gone on the trip with him?"

"Look, I don't know what happened to him," Mitch said gruffly, then turning to Jenna and pointing his finger at her again, adding angrily, "but I know the bites on his hand weren't from that little foxie, and you were there so I want to know what happened!"

"I don't know," she responded, her voice returning to a calm tone as she stared back at Mitch. "Maybe he hurt his own arm more, to make the bite look worse than what my fox did. My fox did bite him hard until he dropped the knife from his hand—I agree with that. You do realize he pulled a knife on us? He was acting crazy, and Ralphie got upset and jumped on his arm." Picking up Ralphie in her arms, she held him close; he was shaking uncontrollably now.

"Don't you need to get home?" Knocker asked, looking at Jenna. "Your mom will be looking for you."

"You're right. It is getting late," Jenna replied, glancing at her watch. Looking back at Mitch, she continued, "I'll let my grandpa know you have not been able to reach Ike. He may want to get the police involved. Thanks for letting us know. Bye."

Jenna handed Ralphie to Knocker so she could stand, then took him back and gave Ralphie a comforting hug. Knocker stood up next to her, and they turned and started walking away.

Mitch called out after them in a menacing tone, "Don't you worry, little lady. I'm not going to stop looking until I find him. Maybe I'll even find that dragon he was bragging about too. Be seeing you around!"

Chapter Five

A Meeting in the Woods

Jenna and Knocker kept walking without looking back, heading to her house.

Grandpa was sitting on the back porch and called out as they entered the back yard. "Hi, everything okay?"

Jenna shook her head and replied, "Hi Grandpa, let's go inside so we can talk."

Once inside, she continued, "We met that guy, Mitch, in the forest, and he's looking for Ike. He hasn't been able to get in touch with him for a few months, and he says he's not leaving until he finds Ike—and Ike's dragon."

Grandpa and Jenna both turned to look at Knocker for his response. Knocker replied, "I did get the feeling that he was going to continue Ike's quest and was not so much looking for Ike himself, but for the dragon Ike was chasing."

"One important thing you need to know, Russ," Knocker said in a serious voice, "Mitch knows the name Knocker. I identified myself as Marcus today, and he asked me if I knew Knocker. He said we looked like we could be related. And if Mitch remembered my name, he may also remember the name Ituria, as I identified myself to him a month ago as Knocker, First Guard to Ituria."

Grandpa nodded. "I understand. This visit from Mitch confirms that the hunters are not done with Middle Forest, and Ike's disappearance seems to have made them curious as to what he really did see."

"Grandpa, I'm worried about my friends," Jenna said, holding Ralphie close. "I'm going out into the back yard to find Sedric and let him know what is going on. He can tell the others in the forest. There aren't supposed to be hunters anymore, but Mitch is back, and I don't trust him. I also told Ralphie he could stay with us as long as he wanted; I don't want him to go through that again, ever!"

"Ralphie, so good to see you!" Grandpa said as he smiled and petted Ralphie gently on the head. "You are always welcome here!"

"Jenna," he continued, "you can go out to the back yard, but please don't wander too far into the forest. Remember Mitch may still be out there, so you need to be able to get back home. I do have a few things to discuss with Knocker, so go ahead and find Sedric. I think that's a good idea. Let him spread the news that there are hunters in Middle Forest!"

"Come on, Ralphie!" Jenna said, trying to be cheerful. "Let's go see how Sedric is doing. I haven't seen him or Fira in a while."

"Okay, Jenna," Ralphie replied nervously, "as long as you carry me. I'm just too scared to be running around in the woods right now. I don't want to get caught in another trap!"

"You got it!" Jenna said, giving him a big hug. "Let's go find your friends. We will let them spread the news, okay? Then you and I will return to the house together and have a snack."

"Jenna," Knocker called to her, "you will need this if you are going to talk with Sedric and the others." He held out his hand and gave her a translation stone. "You have used these before; just remember the range is about ten feet, and in that range, the voice of non-humans you are talking to will be understood by all humans within range of the stone."

"Thanks, Knocker!" Jenna said, putting the translation stone carefully into her pocket so she wouldn't lose it.

Walking through the back yard, Jenna called out for her friend squirrel, "Sedric, are you around? We need to talk!"

"Jenna," Ralphie said anxiously in a low voice, "I hear something a little farther into the forest. It sounds like Sedric, but I'm not sure. It's a warning—loud clicks and caws from several squirrels in the treetops ahead."

On alert now, Jenna wouldn't call out again. Whispering to Ralphie, she asked, "Can you understand what they are saying? Maybe we can get closer and figure out if we can help them."

"Your grandpa said not to go too far into the forest. Maybe we should head back?" Ralphie said, nervously looking back toward Jenna's house.

"Let's just go a little way into the forest, Ralphie," Jenna responded. "I won't go too far, and we'll be able to get back to the house quickly, okay?"

"Okay, if you're sure…" Ralphie started, still worried they wouldn't be able to make it back to the house.

"Shh…" Jenna interrupted in a whisper. "I hear voices. Let's hide behind here; it sounds like someone is walking this way."

Quickly getting off the trail and hiding behind some thick bushes, they heard footsteps coming from opposite directions. Two men were approaching each other on the trail, and it looked like they would meet very near to where Jenna was hiding, crouched close to the ground.

"Don't move!" she whispered urgently to Ralphie as the men got closer.

"Hey, are you Dan?" called a voice from one of the men.

"Yep, are you Mitch?" Dan replied, still suspicious of Mitch's motives. "Why do we have to meet out here in the woods? Why can't we meet in town at my hotel?"

"Because just down the path here is where I saw Ike the last time and also the people I think were involved in his disappearance!" Mitch replied in frustration, pointing directly to Jenna's house. "But they're not saying nothing!"

Holding Ralphie close, Jenna's eyes opened wide as she listened to Mitch, realizing that his plans were aimed directly at her and Grandpa!

Chapter Six

STORIES OF DRAGONS!

"Okay, Mitch, calm down," Dan replied. "I told you I would go on a rescue mission to help you find your friend. That's all I'm here for."

"Oh, I'm okay Dan," Mitch replied in an irritated voice. "I just got done talking to one of the people who saw Ike before he disappeared, a girl named Jenna. I know she was involved in whatever happened to Ike, but she's not talking." His voice got calmer as he focused on Dan's role in his hunt. "Look, I hope the check I sent you cleared and was enough for you to accompany me on my little search. I promise I won't call it a hunt, okay?" Mitch said with a chuckle.

"*And* … I need to talk with you about your trip to North Carolina about a year or so ago." Mitch continued, "I need to ask you some questions."

"Look, Mitch," Dan replied in a tense voice, "like I told you on the phone, I don't want to discuss it. I'm never hunting again. Just leave it at that!"

"Well, Dan, I wanted to know the reason why." Mitch's voice got quieter as he looked around to make sure no one else was on the trail. Jenna peered through the bushes, staying as still as possible. She had to know what Mitch wanted from Dan.

"You wouldn't believe me if I told you, okay?!" Dan said, getting frustrated that Mitch would not take no for an answer.

"Listen," Mitch continued, "did it have any- thing to do with a dragon or kids named Megan and Knocker?" He stopped there to see what Dan would say.

Dan looked at Mitch, his eyes widened, and he looked down to make sure his left sleeve was all the way down on his arm to his wrist and buttoned closed. "What do you mean, a dragon?"

"Well, when I was in the forest you were in—I was trying to catch some of those wolves—I ran into a couple of kids," Mitch continued. "They must have had some type of magic show going on because it appeared one of them turned into a dragon and threatened me. Did that happen to you?"

Dan nervously rubbed the sleeve on his left forearm. "Look, I can't talk about it. They have eyes everywhere. You know that, don't you?"

"Who has eyes everywhere? I need to know. You see, a guy named Ike claimed he had seen a dragon, and I went with him to find it. We didn't find the dragon, but Ike disappeared the next day," Mitch replied. "Now you, *you* didn't disappear, but you gave up your business. Who made you do that?"

"Ituria, that's who—I made a promise to Ituria not to hunt again! There, I said it!" Dan almost yelled at Mitch. "I can never even attempt to hunt again, or they will know!"

"That's the name I heard! What do you know about Ituria? I can't find anything on him or his Island," Mitch said excitedly, leaning in, not wanting to miss a word. "And do you know anything about a teenage boy named Knocker, claims he was First Guard to Ituria? He made me promise not to hunt again." Looking closely at Dan, he continued. "Is that what happened to you?"

"Look, just drop it. I can't talk about it!" Dan said as he started walking away.

Mitch grabbed him by the arm to turn him around. "Look, I think I saw the same dragon that Ike did, and I am going to catch it! If I kill it first, it can't hurt me, right?"

"Did you get a seal from Ituria?" Dan asked slowly. "If you did, how can you be talking like this?"

"I didn't get nothing!" Mitch replied gruffly. "What are you talking about?"

"Then you were lucky!" Dan yelled at him. "I got his seal and can never escape! Look, they can hear and see whatever I do!" Pulling up his left sleeve, he stuck his arm out, revealing a tattoo-like mark on his left forearm. "Look at this!"

Mitch looked at the tattoo on Dan's arm. It was a large capital "I" with a crescent moon through the middle; on the top, there was a drawing of an eye. As he watched in disbelief, the eye appeared to open and look at him. "What… what is going on?" Mitch stammered.

"Yes, they can see and hear you. If you plan on breaking your promise to Knocker not to hunt again, you have just told them so, and they will be looking for you and they will find you!" Dan was hysterical now. "If I do anything connected with hunting, they will capture me and banish me to a deserted island, and I can never return, never see any people ever again, until I die!"

"Dan," Mitch said, not able to accept what Dan was saying, "calm down. This can't be true. How can a tattoo see and hear you? They must be playing on your fears."

"I don't think so, Mitch," Dan replied. "Look at it! Look it in the eye—it stares right back at you!"

"Who is Ituria and how can he be doing this to you?" Mitch wasn't quite convinced this wasn't some elaborate hoax being played on Dan, and Dan was spreading the hoax by showing it to him. "Is he connected to Knocker?"

"Mitch," Dan said anxiously, looking around to see if anyone was watching. "You asked me here to help you find a person. That is all I am willing to do. Anything else, you are on your own. I met Ituria once and that is enough for me!"

"Let's go to my camp, Dan," Mitch replied. "I agree there are too many eyes and ears here out in the open. We can go into my tent. It's just up the trail a bit."

"Don't you get it? It won't matter where I am—they will always hear anything I say, see anything I do!" Dan yelled at Mitch.

"Well, maybe we can trick them at their own game, huh?" Mitch said with a devious look in his eye. "Come on. There's a store in town we can get some paper and pens. No more talking, I agree!"

Chapter Seven

MITCH'S
PLAN EXPOSED

As soon as Dan and Mitch were out of sight, Jenna got up and ran back to the house, holding Ralphie close to her. "Grandpa!" she shouted as she came through the porch door. "Where is Knocker? We need to talk!"

"Jenna, what is the matter? What happened?" Grandpa asked, worried about her sudden return.

"We need to reach Ituria! We need to let him know that Mitch and Dan are working together and will try and conceal their plans from Ituria's seal!" Jenna responded, anxious at what could happen if they were able to trick Ituria.

"Mitch has convinced Dan to try to trick the seal!" Jenna added, her voice stressed. "We need to do something!"

"Jenna, calm down," Grandpa said, walking over and putting his arm around her shoulders. "We will get through this, just like we always do, okay?"

"Okay, Grandpa," Jenna said in a softer voice. "I guess the fact we know Mitch and Dan will be trying to trick Ituria gives us the edge since they don't know we know, right?"

"That's right, Jenna," Grandpa agreed. "Now, tell me exactly what you heard—every detail—so we can be prepared."

"Well," Jenna responded. "Ralphie and I were looking for Sedric, and Ralphie heard a lot of warning calls from the forest. We went in just a little way into the forest to the path and hid when we saw two men walking toward each other, right Ralphie?"

"Yes, we hid and listened to them talking," Ralphie confirmed. "Mitch says he has a camp set up farther into the forest."

Jenna continued as she stroked Ralphie's head. "Dan showed Mitch a tattoo on his arm, which must be Ituria's seal, and he told Mitch it can see and hear anything he says. Dan said he would not go hunting. He's only here to track down Ike."

"Mitch is out to kill the dragon though, he said so—he said to Dan, 'if I kill it, it can't hurt me,'" she added, her voice more stressed as she worried about Knocker. "We need to let Knocker know Mitch is out to kill him!"

"Okay, Jenna, what else did you hear?" Grandpa said. "Anything else we need to know?"

"Yes, Grandpa," she answered, speaking quickly. "Mitch and Dan are going into town to buy some paper and pens. They are going to write down their conversations rather than talk. That way the seal won't be able to hear them."

"Did they say where they were staying?" Grandpa asked.

"Well, like Ralphie said, Mitch has a tent in the forest. I don't know where Dan is staying other than at a hotel—he didn't say which one," Jenna answered. "Why don't I ask Sedric and his friends to locate Mitch's tent? That is probably where he and Dan will base their hunt."

"That's a good idea, Jenna," Grandpa said. "However, you can't go into the forest right now. See if you can get them to come to the edge of the back yard. I don't want you in the forest with Mitch and Dan there. They are dangerous!"

"Okay," Jenna said, glad that she could do something rather than just wait for Mitch and Dan to act. "I'll call to Sedric, to see if he can come over. Ralphie, maybe if you call to him, it will work better since the translation stone only works for about ten feet. Could you do that? I promise you won't have to go into the forest again. We'll stay in our back yard, okay?"

"Yes, I can do that," Ralphie said anxiously. "As long as we don't go back into the forest. I am so scared now the hunters are back."

"Ralphie, I understand, and we will stay in the back yard," Jenna said reassuringly. "If you can call to Sedric and Fira and ask them to come over to us, we can tell them the situation and ask them to go through the trees to see if they can find Mitch or his camp."

"Okay, Jenna," Grandpa said. "Please let Sedric know, then come back and we will decide how best to contact Ituria. Knocker was called away by Ituria, but he said he would be returning soon."

"Ralphie, let's go!" Jenna replied as she carried Ralphie out the porch door and to the back yard. Once they reached the edge of the yard, she continued. "Ralphie, please call to Sedric and ask him to come over. If any of his friends are out there, we can talk to them all."

Ralphie called out to Sedric, "Sedric, Jenna needs to talk to you. Please come over to her home!"

Jenna could hear chattering in the treetops, clicks and ticks of squirrels talking amongst themselves. "Ralphie, what are they saying?"

"Jenna," Ralphie said nervously. "It sounds like Mitch had set several traps out, and Sedric is caught in one of them—he can't get out! His friends are trying to move the trap, so the hunter won't find it!"

"Oh, no!" Jenna cried out, worried for her small friend. "I have to get to him!"

"Jenna, you can't go in there by yourself!" Ralphie answered, trying to reason with her.

"Yes, I must, but you need to go back to the house. First, tell one of the other squirrels to find me. If they get close enough to me, I can understand them," Jenna said quickly. "Please hurry!"

"Julio," Ralphie called out. "Please find Jenna, the human who will be entering the forest! She will help

Sedric—show her where he is! If you get close enough to her, she will understand it when you talk to her!"

Jenna could hear clicking and squeaks in the forest as the squirrels responded to Ralphie.

"Jenna, Julio will be waiting for you," Ralphie said anxiously. "He said to hurry!"

"Thanks, Ralphie, now run back to the house!" Jenna called out as she put him down. "I'm going after Sedric!" Watching Ralphie for a few seconds to make sure he made it to the porch, Jenna turned and ran into the forest to free Sedric.

Chapter Eight

RESCUING SEDRIC

Thinking back to what Mitch and Dan said earlier, Jenna remembered they were going to the store to buy some paper and pens. She should have a few minutes to find Sedric and anyone else who might have been trapped while they were gone.

"Julio!" she called out. "Please find me! I need your help to find Sedric!"

A few minutes into the forest, a squirrel ran up to Jenna and started chattering. "I'm Julio. If you are Jenna, please follow me!"

"Yes, I'm Jenna, I'll follow you!" Jenna replied as she ran after him.

"Here, this way!" Julio said. "The trap is here!"

"I see it, Julio!" Jenna called to him. "Please tell your friends there may be other traps! There is a hunter in the forest, so you are all in danger! If anyone else is caught in a trap, I need to know now!"

"Yes, Jenna," he replied. "I will let them know!" Then he scampered off, chattering to his fellow squirrels.

Reaching down to pick the trap off the ground, Jenna could tell it was designed to catch small animals, as the top and sides were wire mesh. A small squirrel was caught inside, and there was a trail on the ground where his friends dragged the trap through the dirt and leaves.

"Sedric, are you okay?" Jenna whispered to him softly, her voice full of concern. "I will get you out of here as soon as I can!"

"Hi Jenna, thank you!" Sedric said, relief filling his voice as he realized Jenna had come to help him. "I don't know where this came from. We have never seen traps in Middle Forest!"

Looking at the trap, Jenna figured out it was a type of snap trap, and she was able to pull the door open long enough for Sedric to scamper out.

"There you go!" Jenna said to him. "You're free now!"

"Yes!" Sedric answered as he ran to a tree and scurried up the trunk. "Thank you for rescuing me!"

"Please call out to see if anyone else is caught. We only have a few minutes before the hunters return!" Jenna whispered, wanting to make sure no one else was trapped.

Running to the top of the tree, Sedric made a lot of clicking sounds and received numerous responses from various points in the forest. Then he ran back to Jenna. "Jenna, no one else is caught, and everyone is on the alert now!"

"Thanks, Sedric," Jenna responded, glad there were no other animals that needed to be rescued. Putting the trap back on the ground, Jenna walked back toward her house, motioning for Sedric to follow. As they got to the edge of the forest, she stopped and knelt to talk with him.

"Sedric," Jenna said in a low voice, looking around to make sure no one was watching her. "The hunter who was here with Ike is back, and he is looking for the dragon Ike claims to have seen."

"He must be the one who put out these traps, right?" Sedric asked nervously.

"Yes, I think so. You need to warn all your friends throughout Middle Forest about the traps so that they don't get caught," Jenna said. "We also need to locate where Mitch's camp is, so maybe you, Fira, and Julio can organize your friends to check from the trees—don't go on the ground where the traps will be sitting—and let me know if you see any human camps set up. I'll be waiting here in the back yard for any updates. Could you do that?"

"Of course!" Sedric said quickly. "We will check and let you know if we see any tents or firepits or anything. I will tell everyone to stay in the tops of the trees and away from the hunters!"

"Thank you, Sedric!" Jenna whispered. "We need to make sure that Mitch does not find Knocker! That's who he is looking for!"

Scampering up a tree and jumping from branch to branch, he disappeared into the forest. Jenna could hear Sedric calling to his squirrel friends as she sat down in a chair near the edge of the forest to wait for him to return.

About thirty minutes later, Jenna heard the squirrels chattering as they headed her way.

"Jenna, we have found the campsite!" Sedric said as he climbed down the tree and over to where she was sitting.

"How far away is it?" Jenna asked. "Is it along the trail where I can find it?"

"We found it hidden behind a large rock formation near the lake," Sedric said. "Like the hunter was trying to hide from anyone in the forest and maybe spy on the lake area without being seen."

"Okay," Jenna nodded and replied, "it sounds like he is camping near where I rescued Ralphie. I know the spot you are talking about!"

"Also, I saw two humans walking into the camp as we left, so they must be there now!" Sedric said anxiously. "Please don't go there now, okay?"

"Yes, Sedric, I agree we shouldn't go there now; however, do you think this evening you could send Dexter over here so I can talk with him? We will need someone to watch the camp. Maybe he and some of his night friends can help me," Jenna said, working out a plan that wouldn't put her or her friends in danger.

Sedric nodded. "Sure, Jenna. Dexter usually comes out of his home at dusk, right before I go into my nest in the trees. I'll talk to him as soon as he wakes up!"

"Thanks, Sedric!" Jenna replied. "I'll be back at dusk to meet with Dexter!"

Jenna ran back into the house to check on Ralphie and let him know Sedric was safe.

Chapter Nine

PLANS ARE MADE

Running onto the back porch, she looked around for Ralphie. "Ralphie, where are you?" she called out, worried when she couldn't find him.

Grandpa called to her from inside the house. "Jenna, Ralphie is in here!"

"Thank goodness!" Jenna said as she walked quickly inside and went over to give Ralphie a big hug. "Ralphie, so glad you are safe; you need to stay in the house, okay? I was able to get Sedric out of the trap and he is fine, but there are more traps out there."

"Grandpa," Jenna continued, "I am going to meet Dexter at dusk, so we can make plans to spy on Mitch and Dan. We need to know what they are doing, so we can beat them at their own game!"

"You're not going into the forest tonight, are you?" Grandpa asked, worried at what Jenna was planning.

"No, Grandpa," Jenna replied seriously, "but our night friends may be able to give me some clues as to what is going on at the camp."

Pulling out her map of the Frazier conservation area, known to the residents as Middle Forest, Jenna looked at the distance between her house and the rock formations on the east side of the lake. She figured it was less than two miles away.

"Mitch has been here before," she continued, pointing at a spot on the map. "This is where I rescued Ralphie from Ike, and then we headed back this way." Her finger traced the trail through the woods they followed to get back home.

"What I want to know is first, what hotel is Dan staying at, and second, how can we get their notes away from the camp once Mitch leaves in the morning on their 'rescue mission' to hunt Knocker," Jenna said softly, talking to herself.

After thinking for a minute, Jenna asked, "What do you think about this, Grandpa? I'm hoping to ask some of the owls in the vicinity of the lake to help. Maybe Dexter can talk to them for me or bring them to the edge of the forest so I can talk with them."

"If I can get some of the owls to watch and report to Dexter, then Dexter can let me know what is going on," Jenna continued. "I can sit outside tonight and wait for their reports."

"I agree you should be safe here on the porch, Jenna," Grandpa responded, relieved she wouldn't go into the forest at night.

"Okay, Grandpa, but if the owl lets me know Dan is heading for his hotel, I do want to know where he is staying," Jenna replied. "If I can talk to Dan while he is away from Mitch, maybe I can convince him to leave and give up on their hunt for a dragon!"

"How are you going to do that?" Grandpa asked. "We live at least a mile from downtown where the hotels are."

"Well…" Jenna said slowly, still trying to figure out all the contingencies, "there has to be a way. Let me think on it! In the meantime, I'll go out back and wait for Dexter."

Running out the back door, through the porch and to the edge of the back yard, Jenna searched the edge of the forest for Dexter. The sun was setting in the west, so he should be here soon!

Shortly after sunset, a large raccoon popped his head out of the bushes. "Greetings, Jenna!" he called to her. "How can I help?"

"Greetings, Dexter. So good to see you again!" Jenna replied. "I'm hoping you can help me contact your night friends to gather some information. There are human hunters in Middle Forest, and I need to know what building one of them is staying in down in the human buildings; and also, if we can have someone watch the hunter's tent and let me know once the other one leaves in the morning."

"Well," Dexter said, "that sounds like something our friend owls can help with, and they are waking up now also. When I talked to Sedric, he said you might need help watching from the trees, so I stopped and asked two of my friends to stop over when they awoke."

Turning to look into the forest, Dexter continued, "And here they come now! Please let me introduce Alex and Brianna, two owls that live at the top of the tree near my home."

Jenna looked up to see two large owls land on a branch close to her. "Greetings, Alex and Brianna, nice to meet you!"

"Greetings, Jenna," Brianna replied. "Dexter told Alex and I that you are part of Ituria's Alliance, so we will be glad to help you however we can."

"Thank you for your help!" Jenna exclaimed. "We can definitely use it. We have learned there are two hunters who plan on tracking and killing a dragon in Middle Forest, and I need to stop them. We can't let them find Knocker!"

"I agree—we will be..." Alex started but stopped talking and gave Jenna a worried look as he watched Grandpa walked over to join the group.

"No need to worry. This is my grandpa, Russ. He is also part of Ituria's Alliance!" Jenna called to them.

"Greetings, friends of Ituria. I am here to help Jenna on her quest," Grandpa said.

"Greetings, Russ. We are glad to meet you," Alex replied. Then he asked, "Jenna, what can we do to help you?"

"First," Jenna responded, "I need to find out what human building the first hunter is staying in. He will be leaving the second hunter's camp soon. If one of you can follow him and let me know the location of the building—color, size, some shape that distinguishes it from the other buildings—that will help."

Both owls nodded and waited for Jenna to continue. "I also need someone to watch the other hunter still in the camp. He should be there until early morning. Once he leaves camp, there will be some papers inside the tent that I need."

"However," Jenna began with resolve, "I only need you to tell me when he leaves. I do not want you to be put in danger by trying to find the papers. I will do that."

Chapter Ten

NIGHT WATCHERS

"Jenna, do you plan on going to Mitch's camp yourself and searching for the papers?" Grandpa asked, his voice full of concern.

"Yes, Grandpa," Jenna said, nodding to him. "I am the only one who will know what to look for, so I must be the one to search for it." The determination in her eyes showed Grandpa that she had made up her mind. This was something she alone had to do.

"Brianna, I will watch for the human leaving camp tonight," Alex said. "Can you stay until morning and watch for the second human to leave and then let Jenna know?"

"Yes, that's a good plan, Alex!" Brianna replied. "Dexter and Sedric told us where the camp is located, so we will be off now to watch the camp. We will report as the information is available, Jenna!"

"Thank you, Alex and Brianna," Jenna called to them. "I will await here for your reports!"

Jenna sat on the porch waiting for the owls to report back. About forty-five minutes later, the hoot of an owl announced Alex's return as he appeared in a tree in the back yard. Jumping up to meet him, she went out the porch door and ran over to the tree. "What have you learned, Alex?" she called out as she got closer.

"I saw one man leave the tent and followed him to the human buildings," Alex answered. "He went into the third large building on the north side of your road; it had three large circles on a sign in front of it. He went in and I waited a few moments to make sure he did not leave again. Then I flew here to report."

"Thank you!" Jenna responded. "From your description, I know what building he went into, and I will be able to find it in the morning. My deepest gratitude to you and Brianna for your help. I will wait here for her return. Thank you again for your help, Alex. Take care!"

Jenna and Grandpa stayed on the porch, waiting for Brianna's report. Ralphie was on the porch also, and after making a bed for Ralphie out of an old blanket, Jenna brought him some food and water. Everyone settled in for the night, waiting for Brianna to return to let them know when Mitch was on the prowl. While waiting, Jenna grabbed her backpack and put a few items in it just in case she needed to leave quickly in the morning.

"Jenna," Grandpa said once they were settled in, "I talked with Ituria about Mitch, and he doesn't want him in Middle Forest. Even as a tree, Mitch might find a way to hurt his friends. Nor will he agree to have Mitch exiled to the moon. Ituria is working with Knocker, who should be back some-time tomorrow morning, and Ituria offered another solution."

"What is his solution, Grandpa?" Jenna asked. "I don't want to kill Mitch—even though he would have no problems killing us or Knocker, but we can't have him hunting here in Middle Forest anymore."

"Well, Ituria said that he would give you a potion to turn Mitch into a sea creature who could never come back to Middle Forest," Grandpa replied, handing her a small vial. "Ituria said that if you can get Mitch to swallow this potion, it will turn him into a shark, and then Knocker can fly him to the ocean. Mitch can take his chances with all the other hunters in the sea. Does that sound like something you can do?"

"I will have to work out a plan, Grandpa, but Knocker has to stay away until the transformation is almost complete!" Jenna replied seriously as she took the potion and slipped it into her backpack. "Please tell Knocker to stay away until I call for him. I can't let Mitch see him before he is given the magic potion."

"Agreed, Jenna. I will let him know," Grandpa said.

They both settled in to wait for Brianna to return in the morning, and Jenna was already making plans on what she would need to do at her meeting with Mitch the next day.

After she slept lightly on and off through the night, the hooting of an owl woke Jenna up. Glancing around, she saw Grandpa and Ralphie were still sleeping on the porch, so she quietly went into the back yard looking for the source of the call and saw Brianna in a tree close to the house.

"Greetings, Brianna," Jenna called softly, not wanting to wake the others. "Any news for us?"

"Greetings, Jenna," Brianna replied. "I saw the second man leaving the tent. He had some boxes and chains with him. I watched him for a few minutes, and he was leaving the boxes and chains in various areas in Middle Forest. He was heading in this direction; you need to be aware he may be here soon!"

"Thank you, Brianna!" Jenna said, looking first into the woods and then back at Grandpa and Ralphie sleeping on the porch. "Thank you for your help, and we will heed your warning! Take care!"

Running back onto the porch, Jenna whispered to Grandpa as she gently touched his shoulder, "Grandpa, wake up! Brianna says Mitch is heading this way!"

"What . . . oh, Jenna, what's going on?" Grandpa said, still a little groggy from sleep.

"Brianna said Mitch is out laying traps now, Grandpa, and he's heading this way!" Jenna whispered urgently. "I need to go to his tent while he is out, and you need to protect Ralphie, okay?"

"Wait, wait, Jenna," Grandpa replied. "We don't know where Mitch is, right? Only that he is wandering the forest and coming in our direction. You can't meet him in the forest alone!"

"What's going on?" Ralphie said sleepily as he awoke.

"Mitch is out laying traps, Ralphie, so you need to stay with Grandpa, okay?" Jenna answered.

"Yes, I will stay here," Ralphie replied anxiously, now wide awake.

"Grandpa, I will go around Mitch and search his tent before he gets back. If he does show up here, maybe you can stall him for a few minutes." Jenna was running the many things she had to accomplish this morning through her head. "Don't worry about me. Once I find the notes, I'm going to head over to the hotel where Dan went and wait for him in the lobby before he heads back to Mitch's tent. I'll try to convince him to leave, okay?"

"Jenna," Grandpa replied, worried for her safety. "Are you sure you want to go out there? Knocker and Ituria are not in the forest until later this morning. They won't be able to help you."

"Grandpa, I'll be fine," Jenna said as she walked over to Ralphie, resting her hand on his head. "I need you to make sure that Mitch doesn't get Ralphie. I've been working out the other…"

A clanking noise from the back yard caused them to turn. It was Mitch emerging out of the forest, still carrying half a dozen traps!

"Grandpa!" Jenna whispered urgently. "I'm going out the front, so Mitch won't see me. Just protect Ralphie, please!" Jenna grabbed her backpack and raced into the house, hoping Mitch had not seen her on the porch.

Chapter Eleven

MITCH VISITS GRANDPA

Jenna left quietly through the front door and crept into the forest, making sure she was out of Mitch's view. She paused behind some large trees to listen to what Mitch wanted, in case she had to step in and help Grandpa. She didn't trust Mitch.

"Hey, Grandpa!" Mitch shouted out jokingly as he came into the back yard.

"Hello, do I know you?" Grandpa replied in a serious tone, standing up on the porch and motioning for Ralphie to lay on the floor so Mitch couldn't see him.

"Yes, I was here a few months ago. Don't you remember?" Mitch answered, advancing farther into the back yard.

"Funny you should be coming in through my back yard this early in the morning. Is there something wrong? Do I need to call the police?" Grandpa asked.

"No, no!" Mitch answered quickly. "I was just in the woods back here and saw you on the porch and thought I would drop by. Do you remember me? I'm the one who kept Ike from hurting your little grand-daughter, remember?"

"Well, I do remember Ike being here a few months ago. Were you part of the group that took him back to your camp?" Grandpa asked, wanting to know how much Mitch was going to reveal, not wanting to volunteer anything.

"You bet I was," Mitch replied, boastful of his role in protecting Jenna. "If it weren't for me, Ike might have hurt your little granddaughter. By the way, where is she now? I had a few questions for her."

"She's sleeping now; it is rather early in the morning," Grandpa replied, irritated at the request. "You'll have to come back later in the day, and please don't come through the back yard anymore. That could be considered trespassing, okay?" Grandpa turned to go into the house, but Mitch wasn't done yet.

"Hey, mind if I join you on the porch?" Mitch asked.

"Yes, I do mind," Grandpa replied in an irritated voice. "This is way too early to have company. If there is a problem we need to address, please let me know now; otherwise, I'm going inside to get break-fast ready before the family wakes up." There was no way he was letting Mitch onto the porch.

"Well, if you could give me a few minutes, please!" Mitch called back as he stopped walking toward the house. "I'm looking for Ike; he seems to have disap-peared. Do you know where he is?"

"Ike? I thought you took him out of the forest with you. Last thing I remember, your group was looking for him and came by here. Didn't you find him?" Grandpa asked.

"Well, no, we didn't, and you seemed to have known him for a long time, Grandpa, and I was wondering if he had ever come back to talk with you," Mitch replied, pressing Grandpa for answers.

"No, Ike and I don't agree on many things, so I doubt he would have been wanting to talk to me again. And my name is Russ. You are not my grandson, so I am not your grandfather, okay?" Grandpa responded curtly, annoyed at Mitch's condescending behavior.

"Oh, sorry about that," Mitch replied, still in an arrogant tone. "Well, Russ, how did you come to meet Ike?"

"By the way, what's your name?" Grandpa asked. "I don't think you have identified yourself to me yet."

"I'm Mitch!" Mitch replied. "You mean you don't remember me?"

"Well, there were four men with Ike. That's all I remember. What's your last name, Mitch?"

"Oh, you don't need that!" Mitch said with a half-hearted laugh. "We're comrades—hunters—first names are fine!"

"I am not a hunter, Mitch, and never was a hunter like Ike was. Are you a professional hunter like Ike?" Grandpa asked angrily.

Suddenly, Mitch's attitude changed. "Why do you want to know, huh?" he asked defensively.

"Well, you come into my back yard in the early morning, and you are carrying traps. What do you want me to think? And what are you doing here? The forest you came out of is a wildlife refuge, a no-hunt zone. You know that, right?" Grandpa responded, his voice getting louder as he challenged Mitch to explain why he was there.

"Well, I found these traps in the woods. Someone else must have left them," Mitch replied as he started to back away from the house. "I was gathering them up to make sure none of the little animals got caught. I know this is a no-hunting zone."

This was Jenna's cue to head out on her task. Grandpa had the upper hand in this conversation now, so Jenna headed to Mitch's camp. She could hear Grandpa and Mitch arguing as she went farther into the forest. She had to find the notes before he got back!

Chapter Twelve

SEARCH FOR
THE NOTES

J enna jogged toward where she thought Mitch's camp was located. The tent would be hidden, so once she got close, she slowed to a walk and started looking behind the large boulders that surrounded one portion of the lake where Sedric said the tent was located.

Loud clicking could be heard as she rounded one turn on the trail, causing her to look up into the trees. Her friend squirrels were clicking and twitching their tails; she was almost there! She followed them and found her way to the campsite, looking around carefully to make sure no one was near to see her. She would only have a few minutes for the search, so as soon as she felt the area was safe, she entered the tent.

There was not much in the tent, a cot with a blanket and pillow, along with two small boxes that looked like ammunition, as well as a few bags that contained food and water. There was a notepad laying on top of the bed, but there was nothing written inside. *Where would someone hide their notes?*

Jenna first searched the cot, looking into the pillowcase, under the pillow and blanket, but found nothing. She went over to the bags of food. Maybe it had been stuck in there. Quickly emptying and refilling the bags, she found nothing there either. Okay, she was running out of time—what about the ammo boxes?

As Jenna bent over to pick up one of the boxes, she noted that some of the dirt on the ground near them had been disturbed. After emptying the ammo boxes into her backpack and putting the empty boxes back where they were, she started brushing the dirt away. The top of a jar lid appeared!

Sounds from outside caught her attention. The squirrels were clicking loudly, that must mean that Mitch was close! Digging quickly to grab the jar, she stuffed it into her backpack and put the dirt back into the hole so there was no evidence that the jar was missing. Then she did a quick look around to make sure everything was where it had been and headed out of the tent. As she stepped out, Sedric ran up to her and whispered anxiously, "Jenna, he is almost back. You must leave!"

Nodding her head, Jenna took off, away from the path that Mitch would follow to get back to his tent. That meant she was heading away from home and town, but she needed to make sure Mitch did not see her. Once she was far enough way, Jenna circled around to head back home. But first, she had to know what Mitch and Dan had discussed, what their plans really were!

Sitting down and pulling the jar from her backpack, she saw it indeed held a folded piece of paper. Quickly, she opened the lid to read the contents, knowing that anything she learned would help her to protect Knocker.

Did you see a dragon on your last hunt?

Yes.

Do you know Knocker?

Yes! he is the dragon I saw.

I talked with Knocker too – he says he works for someone named Ituria. Do you know who Ituria is?

Ituria is a unicorn! I saw him - he burned this seal on my arm with his horn.

Is Marcus related to Knocker – they look similar?

<u>Marcus is Knocker</u>! Marcus is the name he uses when

he looks like a human. How can we get Knocker?

Get Jenna's pet fox. She will look for him, then we can trap her too.

Why, what does she know?

I saw her talking with Marcus earlier today, she must know he is a dragon! Even if she doesn't know, if we grab her, then he will try and rescue her, and we will get him either way

I can't be hunting - what do I say if someone asks why I have a gun?

Tell them it is for protection from dangerous animals

What do I say we are doing in the woods? Anyone asks, we are on a rescue mission, looking for a friend who disappeared, Ike Monnihan — they do not need to know we are hunting a dragon

Didn't you make a promise to Knocker that you

would not hunt again?
Yeah, so what?

Do you really want to break your promise to a dragon?
Well, if I get him first, what difference does it make?

What if you don't get him first? Let's just make sure I do, okay?

Meet me here at 10:00 tomorrow morning and we'll go looking for Ike and the dragon. Not earlier, I have some traps out now, and I need to check them first thing in the morning – need to make sure I have something to show for the trip! *Okay, I'll be back here at 10:00 tomorrow morning*

It was clear that Mitch and Dan would be hunting Knocker, and they would try to capture Ralphie and Jenna as bait!

Looking at her watch, Jenna noted that it was almost 9:00 a.m. now. She would have to go to Dan's hotel before he left, so she needed to get there by 9:30 a.m. She started jogging toward town; she had to hurry!

Chapter Thirteen

CONFRONTING DAN

Jenna reached Dan's hotel at 9:25 a.m.; she made it! Now, all she had to do was to wait for him to leave and talk him out of joining Mitch's dragon hunt. She took a minute to catch her breath, then stepped into the lobby and looked around. Waiting in the lobby wouldn't guarantee she would see Dan, so she stood just outside the front entrance. This way she could also see the parking lot and the side entrances; she couldn't take the chance of missing him.

She had seen Dan yesterday, so she would recognize him, but he hadn't seen her, so he wouldn't run away if he saw her. Pretending to be doing something with the items in her backpack, she took a quick glance around every few seconds to see if there were any people leaving the hotel. About five minutes later, she saw Dan exit through a side door and head to the parking lot.

Jenna ran over to him before he could reach his car and asked calmly, "Dan, are you sure you want to do this?"

"What do you mean? Who are you?" Dan replied, getting a little nervous, glancing around to see who else was there.

"I am part of Ituria's Alliance, and I know you are planning to join Mitch on a hunt today. Are you sure you want to do this?" Jenna asked again.

"What… no, I'm not!" Dan replied angrily. "I'm just going out for breakfast!"

"You're not going to meet Mitch at 10:00 at his camp?" Jenna asked.

"What do you mean?" Dan asked, shocked that she would know that. "I never said I was going to meet Mitch at 10:00. I'm going out for breakfast now!"

He tried to move past her to get to his car, but she jumped in front of him again and reached into her backpack for the notes she found at Mitch's camp.

"So, isn't this your writing?" Jenna asked, showing him the paper. "Do you need me to read to you where you agreed to meet Mitch to go on a hunting trip?"

"Who are you?" Dan shouted. "How did you get that?" He made a quick grab to take the note back, but Jenna jumped back before he could reach it.

"I'm part of Ituria's Alliance. And like you told Mitch yesterday when you met in the woods, we can see and hear everything," Jenna replied. "You didn't think writing it down would keep us from knowing, did you?"

"Look little girl," Dan argued. "I'm not hunting anything. I'm going to help Mitch find an old friend of his, okay?"

"Changing the name of your search from hunting to a rescue mission still doesn't change *what* you are doing," Jenna said, getting a little defiant, letting Dan know that she wasn't buying his story. "Mitch is hunting for a dragon, and whatever else he can get, and you are there to help him. It's all written down, including that Mitch intends to kill whatever he finds!"

"Dan," Jenna continued with resolve, "be careful what you say because you know they are listening. We knew that you weren't planning on helping Mitch with his hunt when you came into town. Mitch is out there now setting up traps, even though he also made a promise never to hunt again."

Stopping to quickly put the notes back into her backpack, she continued. "If you leave now, Ituria will not find that you have broken your promise to him; however, if you go into the forest to meet Mitch, your promise is deemed broken, with all the consequences that entails. Please consider your actions wisely." Standing still, Jenna watched Dan as he tried to figure out what he should be doing, how he should react.

"I didn't do anything wrong! I didn't even bring a gun!" Dan shouted at her.

"That is why Ituria is giving you a chance to back away and go home now," Jenna responded. "If you go into the forest, you are agreeing to join Mitch on his hunt, and you will have broken your promise."

Looking around to see if anyone else was close enough to hear the conversation, Dan said in an anxious voice, "So, if I go home now, Ituria won't send Knocker after me?"

"That is correct, Dan. At this point in time, you have not broken your promise," Jenna confirmed. "However, if you decide to join Mitch on his hunt, then Knocker will return to take you to your banishment."

"Well… what about Mitch?" Dan asked, still not sure which path he would follow.

"Mitch has already broken his promise. He will not get the same chance. That's why I came to you first," Jenna replied. "Ituria will deal with him, and Ituria does not have patience for humans who break their promises. Mitch may get what he wished for, to join Ike." Jenna paused for a moment, then added quietly, "I know what happened to Ike, and you do not want to suffer the same fate."

"Okay, you win!" Dan said, now in a panic. "I'm going to pack up and leave." Starting to walk quickly back to the hotel, he continued, "You don't have to tell me again. I'm out of here."

"Thank you, Dan. I will let Ituria know. Remember, we can always see and hear you, even if you write it down!" Jenna called out to him. "Do not test us again!"

As Dan headed into the hotel, Jenna turned and started jogging toward Mitch's camp. It was going to be close, and she was not sure if she would make it by 10:00 a.m.

Chapter Fourteen

MEETING WITH MITCH

Lifting the tent door flap up, Jenna walked into Mitch's tent. Mitch was bending down looking at something on the ground and didn't look up. "You're late!" he called out in an irritated voice. "Where have you been?"

"I've been talking to Dan," Jenna replied.

Mitch stood and spun around, surprised that Jenna was in the tent rather than Dan. "What are *you* doing here?" he demanded in a gruff voice.

"Like I said, I've been talking to Dan," Jenna repeated. "You should know that he's decided not to break his promise to Ituria and is heading home now, so don't expect him to show up for your meeting this morning."

"Well, little girl," Mitch said in a menacing voice, "you were the one I was looking for anyway, so that's just fine." Mitch walked over to Jenna and stood in front of her with a mean scowl on his face. "Now, you better tell me what happened to Ike, okay?"

Jenna did not back away. She just looked at him and said confidently, "I do know what happened to Ike. Do you want to go see him?"

"What?" Mitch asked in disbelief. "You mean he is still here?" For a second, Mitch's eyes opened wide, but soon his brows furrowed again, and the frown returned.

"Yes, he is. Ike promised me he would not hunt anymore, and then he tried to kill my grandfather and my fox just to get to me. He broke his promise to me," Jenna added with conviction, letting Mitch know his threatening behavior really didn't affect her.

"Speaking of promises, didn't you also promise not to hunt anymore, just about a month ago, wasn't it?" Jenna asked, then waited for Mitch's reply.

Mitch stared at Jenna for a few moments, trying to figure out how she knew. Then he responded, "Look, I'm not hunting. I'm here looking for Ike. What makes you think I'm hunting?" Mitch asked defensively.

"Well, it could be all the traps we saw you leave in the forest, for one thing," she replied.

"No, no… you got that wrong." Mitch said with a fake laugh, then continued lying to defend his actions. "Actually, you see, I was picking them up. I know this forest is a no-hunt zone, and I was protecting the little animals."

"Mitch, we saw you leaving them in the forest," Jenna answered curtly, irritated at Mitch's lies. "I had to free a friend of mine from one of your traps yesterday. I hate to think what would have happened if you had gotten to him."

Jenna looked around the tent, she noted the dirt where the jar had been buried had not changed, so Mitch may not be aware she had the notes. Looking back at him, she asked angrily, "And why were you going to trap my pet fox? I would like you to explain that one. Didn't he go through enough with Ike trapping him?"

"What makes you think I was looking for your fox?" Mitch asked.

"Well, that's what you told Dan yesterday," Jenna replied. "And just so you know, calling your trip a rescue mission doesn't change the fact that you were going to kill whatever you were hunting for, does it?" Jenna said loudly as she abruptly turned and walked outside the tent.

"Now just a second," Mitch yelled at her as he followed her outside, "where are you getting all these wild ideas? Who said I was going to kill anything? I'm just looking for Ike!"

"Look Mitch, if you are really looking for Ike, I can take you to see him since he is still here in the forest," Jenna said, pointing toward the trail leading to Ike.

"You bet I want to see him!" Mitch said gruffly. "Let's go!"

"One thing, though," Jenna added, returning to her calm demeanor, and looking Mitch in the eyes. "You will need to leave all your weapons here in the tent: no guns, no knives, no anything. Do you agree to that?" she asked and waited for his reply.

"Why should I do that? What if some wild animal attacks me?" Mitch responded, not sure if he wanted to go anywhere without his weapons.

"I can guarantee that nothing will attack you in this forest, as long as you have no weapons, okay? If you do have weapons, I cannot promise that you will be safe. If you want to see Ike, that is my only condition. No weapons are allowed where Ike is staying," Jenna replied confidently. "All weapons must remain here in your tent; they will be here when you get back."

Mitch stared at Jenna for a second, then asked in a menacing tone, "What if I don't agree?"

"Then you will never see Ike again," Jenna said without emotion. "It is your choice. I don't want to have to worry about you pulling a knife on me while we are in the forest."

"Well," Mitch's voice turned mean as he put his hand on his back pocket, "what if I pull a knife on you now? What if I *make* you take me to Ike?"

"Won't work, Mitch," Jenna said, still standing confidently in front of him. "Ike tried pulling a knife on me too, and it didn't work out so well for him."

Jenna could see Mitch was thinking about how to proceed, not sure which way was better. "Okay, little girl. Deal!" he said begrudgingly. "But you better be telling me the truth when you say you know where Ike is!"

"I am telling you the truth, Mitch. Go put all your weapons in your tent, and then come back, and we will head over to Ike," Jenna said calmly, moving a little farther down the trail. "He's not that far away."

Chapter Fifteen

FINDING IKE

Jenna started walking down the trail, and Mitch caught up with her after a quick trip to his tent.

"By the way, Jenna, where is your friend, Marcus?" Mitch asked, trying to sound friendly. "Is he still here?"

"No, he was staying with us for a few days while his family went on a business trip, and he's left this morning. Why?" Jenna responded evenly.

"No reason," Mitch said slowly. "Dan said he met Marcus. Did you know that?"

"Did he?" Jenna replied. "Where did he meet him?"

"Oh, it doesn't matter," Mitch replied, but Jenna could tell he was thinking, trying to piece everything together.

"Did Dan ever meet Knocker, that other guy you were looking for?" Jenna asked. "Is that where you got the name? Or did you meet Knocker yourself? How did you get that name?"

"Well, I did meet Knocker once, only for a few minutes though," Mitch said warily. "We had a short discussion, and then he left again."

"Oh, okay," Jenna replied, trying to get Mitch to say more. "What did you discuss?"

"None of your business!" Mitch snapped.

"Well, Dan said you promised Knocker you wouldn't hunt again. Is that right?" Jenna asked, keeping her voice calm, not allowing herself to react to Mitch's ever-changing attitude.

"Why would he tell you that? Huh?" Mitch replied gruffly. "He should know better!"

"Well, did you?" Jenna asked again. "It is kind of important I know what you told Knocker. Did you promise him you would never hunt again? That was the same promise Ike gave me." Jenna stopped walking and turned to look at Mitch, waiting for an answer.

"None of your business, okay!" Mitch yelled and then went silent, continuing to walk down the trail.

"Ike is right up here, right by where you found his knife," Jenna said as she followed behind him, pointing to a large tree along the trail.

"Okay, well, where is he?" Mitch asked, looking around. There was nothing but the trail and trees in both directions.

"He is right here," Jenna said, walking over to within a foot of Ike and pointing to the tree. "This is Ike—he was transformed into this tree. In this forest, we do not kill unless necessary, so this was his fate, as decided by Ituria."

Walking around the area, Jenna pointed out the remains of an old campfire. "This is where Ike held my grandpa and Ralphie hostage, waiting for me to rescue them. He was planning on killing me, too. He said none of us would survive the night." Turning to look at Mitch again, she continued, "By the way, I'm the one who threw his knife into the fire."

"Listen, kid, this isn't funny!" Mitch yelled angrily. "You said you would show me where Ike was. Now you are giving me some nonsense that you turned him into a tree. Come on!"

Jenna looked up at the tree. The branches weren't moving. It looked like all the other trees. "While this may look like the other trees, it really is Ike. He is probably too embarrassed to acknowledge what happened."

"Ike," Jenna called out, "Mitch doesn't believe I turned you into a tree. We both know what happened, though, don't we? Should Mitch suffer the same fate? He's back, not really looking for you, although that is what he claims, but really hunting for your dragon!"

Mitch stared at the tree, half thinking the tree would start talking to him, but nothing happened. "Listen, little girl, this has gone far enough!"

"Mitch, why don't you use your knife to make a small cut into the bark of the tree? That should get his attention," Jenna asked, still looking at the tree.

"But you told me not to bring any knives, remember?" Mitch said slyly, not wanting to reveal he still had a knife.

"Well, you've lied about everything else. Why should I trust that you would honor your word not to bring a weapon?" Jenna retorted. "I know you brought a knife with you. I saw it in your back pocket a few minutes ago. Now, if Ike won't answer you, you may have to threaten him with your knife."

"One thing you have to know, though," Jenna continued seriously as she turned to look at Ike, "is that Ike won't be able to actually talk to you—he can move his branches a bit and possibly drop some leaves if you get him mad enough. That's about all he can do now. Cutting the bark with your knife will be the same as cutting his skin, though, and he will feel the pain of your cut, so just a small scratch will suffice."

As Jenna finished talking, the leaves in the Ike tree started rustling as the ends of the branches started moving slightly. Jenna pointed to the leaves moving.

"That was just the wind, little girl!" Mitch yelled at her, pulling out his knife.

"No, it wasn't. Look at the other trees—there is no wind. That was Ike," Jenna said, retaining her quiet demeanor, but backing up just a bit. "If you don't believe me, try it!"

"Well, I will! And once I prove you are lying, we'll see what happens to you!" Mitch yelled at her as he walked over to the tree that was Ike.

As he put his hand on the trunk of the tree, the whole tree shuddered, and several leaves fell on and around Mitch. Mitch looked up at the tree and then at the leaves that had fallen.

"Ike doesn't want you to cut him, Mitch," Jenna said quietly. "Did you feel him shudder? He is scared of you."

"You're just making it all up, little girl!" Mitch yelled at her. "I'll show you!"

Mitch used his knife to make a large gash in the tree trunk, knocking off several pieces of bark. As he backed away, a red liquid started oozing from the gash. The tree shuddered again, and the branches started drooping down.

"Well, I guess you gave Ike just as much respect as you give any other living creature," Jenna replied, her anger beginning to show in her voice. "And he did feel that. Look at the large gash you made. Does it make you feel good to know that you finally found Ike and first thing you did was to hurt him like that?"

Getting farther from Mitch, who was still holding the knife in his hand, Jenna continued Ike's story. "This was the only option left to me. Ike said he would never leave us alone. He laughed at me because I didn't want to kill him—and this is where he ended up." Jenna stopped to point at the Ike tree. The wound in the tree was still oozing red sap, now dripping down the trunk of the tree.

Jenna's voice conveyed quiet confidence as she looked at Mitch. "Mitch, you also pose a threat to me, my family, and my friends. Now, I will have to decide what will happen to you."

Chapter Sixteen

MITCH FIGHTS BACK

"**Y**ou don't scare me, little girl!" Mitch yelled at her, waving his knife, dripping with the red sap.

"You don't scare me either," Jenna said fearlessly, "even with your little knife. In my forest, we do not kill unless it is necessary; there are always other ways to solve a problem. Take Ike as an example—his arrogance did not help him, did it, Ike?"

Jenna and Mitch both looked at the tree as its leaves started rustling and a low moaning sound could be heard resonating through the trunk and branches.

"Well, I'm not Ike, and you won't trick me like you tricked him," Mitch uttered angrily as he took a step toward Jenna. "I know that you know Knocker, that he is a dragon, and he lives here, so I'm going to make you take me to him. Got it?"

"Are you sure you want that?" Jenna replied. "From what I understand, you made a promise to Knocker never to hunt again, and yet you are hunting him. That sounds like a broken promise to me. Do you really want a dragon to punish you for your broken promise?"

Mitch stopped for a moment, and then replied in a falsely friendly voice, "Look, I'm not hunting him. Where did you get that idea? I just want to see him. I heard he was a ferocious dragon, but I never did see him as a dragon."

"You told Dan you were going to find him and kill him, so doesn't that sound like you are hunting him?" Jenna countered, angry that Mitch was lying to her again. "We know what you and Dan said—and wrote—to each other. You can't keep secrets from Ituria; that's why Dan went away."

"What did you do to Dan? Why did he leave?" Mitch yelled at her. "I paid him good money to come out here, and you made him leave without completing his job! I figure you owe me for that!"

"Dan has decided to honor his promise to Ituria and Knocker. He has returned home and has been warned not to associate with dishonorable people like you again," Jenna responded quietly, conveying to Mitch she was not impressed with him and his threats. "I wouldn't try talking to him again, it won't do you any good. And … I'm not sure you will get the chance."

"What do you mean I won't get the chance?" Mitch yelled at her. "There's nothing you can do to me; I can leave whenever I want!"

"Can you?" Jenna asked confidently. "Well, then why don't you leave?"

"Because you still have to show me where Knocker is—that's why!" Mitch said furiously.

"Look, there is no dragon here for you to hunt," Jenna said. She could feel her anger rising within her. "You need to just leave. If he was here, he would punish you for breaking your promise! And yes, he is a ferocious dragon, but we sent him away! You will not get the chance to hunt him!"

"I never said I was going to hunt him. You can't prove I broke any promise!" Mitch replied, trying to intimidate Jenna, but it didn't work.

"Yes, Mitch, I can," Jenna responded with resolve, knowing she was in control of the situation.

Mitch stopped and stared at her, his eyes widened for just a moment, worried that he might have been caught in his lies.

Reaching into her backpack, she pulled out the notes she found in Mitch's tent, and with it the little vial of potion, quickly slipping the vial into her pocket. Holding up the notes, she said in a harsh voice, "*Your* words in *your* handwriting say you were going to hunt Knocker and 'get him first.' Do you not consider those words to mean you are hunting and will kill him when you find him? If that is not what you meant, now is your chance to explain."

Jenna glared at Mitch, waiting for him to respond, but there was no answer from Mitch. "Your silence is an admission of your guilt!" Jenna said angrily. "You will not honor your promise to Knocker!"

Looking at the notes he and Dan wrote, Mitch realized that she could use them against him. But his worry didn't last long. His face got mean again, and a nasty smile appeared on his face. "Well, little girl, I have you now. He will have to come rescue you, and then I will kill him too!" Mitch laughed and pointed the knife at her.

"This is my forest!" Jenna shouted at him. "There is no dragon here for you to hunt—you must deal with me! Ike was very arrogant, especially when he heard me say that I would not kill him, and he said he would never leave me or my grandpa alone, but his arrogance did not help him. Look where it landed him! Do you want to end up as a tree, too?"

"No, I don't think so, little girl!" Mitch yelled back as he got into an attack stance, pointing his knife at her, ready to strike. "This time the hunter wins!"

As he started to attack, Jenna knew she had waited long enough. She had given Mitch a chance to leave, but he wouldn't stop. She knew what she had to do.

She let her emotions take control, feeling the transformation start, and as she turned into a large white wolf, she leaped at Mitch and grabbed the hand with the knife with her wolf teeth, biting hard until he dropped the knife. He cried out in pain as he fell back onto the ground. As she stood over him, she growled, "As I told you before, that didn't work for Ike either!"

Chapter Seventeen

MITCH'S FATE

J enna's translation stone was in her pants pocket, which became part of her wolf body as she transformed into a white wolf, so she knew that Mitch would understand her. At this point, Mitch just stared at her with a blank face, eyes wide and mouth gaping, not believing what he was seeing. With her wolf fangs close to his face, she growled ominously, "This is my forest. We have other ways to deal with humans who have no honor!"

Knowing she had to act quickly, Jenna closed her eyes for a few seconds to calm herself and transformed back into a human. Pulling the vial from her pocket, she quickly opened it and poured the contents down Mitch's throat before he realized what was happening, then she backed away before he could react.

"What… what are you doing?!" Mitch said in a daze as he tried to scoot away, then he tried to cough out the liquid. But was too late; the potion had already run down his throat.

Now Mitch's hunting instinct kicked in. He became alert and needed to assess his current situation. He looked at his hand; it was bleeding from several punctures and rips caused by Jenna's wolf teeth. "So," he yelled at her, "you did bite Ike! He *was* telling the truth!"

Then he was silent, his eyes darting around the area, trying to figure out what he could do to take control of the situation, searching for where the knife ended up. He wasn't going to give up so easily!

Jenna moved farther away from Mitch, leaving him sitting on the ground holding his wounded hand. She saw the knife had landed several feet away from Mitch, just out of his reach. Quickly grabbing it before he could, she put it into her backpack. He wouldn't be able to use it to threaten her again!

"You pose a problem to my forest," she yelled at him defiantly as she stood in front of him, still sitting on the ground. "I do not want you here. Even as a tree, you may find a way to hurt my friends. Ituria does not want you banished to his Island. You are totally without honor, as you not only broke your promise to Knocker, but you also tried to get Dan to break his promise to Ituria."

"You will never return to my forest, Mitch!" Jenna continued. "You will never threaten me or my friends again, do you understand?"

Mitch looked at her for a few seconds, his eyes wide, not sure what he could believe anymore. He needed to get away, get to his tent with his weapons, then he would return to answer her. He stood and started running down the trail toward his campsite.

"Mitch," Jenna shouted after him, "I wouldn't run too far if I were you, or your transformation will result in your death!"

Stopping and turning around to look at Jenna, he yelled furiously, "What do you mean? What transformation?"

"The liquid I poured into your mouth was a magical elixir that will allow you to hunt for the remainder of your life, as that appears to be your main goal," Jenna yelled back. "However, it will also pit you against some of the most cunning hunters in the world, hunters who are also ready and willing to kill, and you will have to kill to keep yourself alive."

"This is just another one of your stories, right? Just like Ike is a tree!" Mitch said angrily as he turned to leave again, holding his wounded hand close to his chest.

"No, Mitch," Jenna shouted out, "once you transform, you will only have a few minutes to be transported to your new home. You are probably already feeling the changes take place—look at your hands!"

Looking down at his hands, he gasped as he saw them transforming into grey shark fins; the bite marks showing up on his right fin. "What have you done?!" he cried out in panic. "What have you done to me?!"

"You are unable to keep your promises and want to hunt and kill without reason," Jenna answered. "Now you will be hunting every day, but you will need to hunt and kill to survive. You will have no choice. Know that you will also be hunted by others."

As she watched Mitch fall to the ground, his feet and legs transforming into a large shark tail, she continued. "Yes, you are being transformed into a shark. You will have a fair chance to live out your life in the ocean and use your hunting skills to survive."

"As a shark, all other creatures will know immediately that you are dangerous. You can't lie and cheat you way out of problems," Jenna said as she walked over to him. "At least sharks have honor. They do not pretend or lie. They do what they have done for millions of years to survive."

Laying on the ground, Mitch's body had transformed into a shark, only his head remained human. Jenna watched as the grey sharkskin crept up his shoulders and to his neck. Soon the transformation would be complete!

"Knocker," Jenna called out into the forest, "it is done!"

In response to her call, Knocker walked out of the forest in his human form. "Greetings Jenna, you have done well!"

"Thank you, Knocker," Jenna replied. "Can you please take Mitch to the ocean so that he does not suffocate here on land? Once he has totally transformed, he will only have a few minutes to get to water."

"I will be glad to do so. You no longer have to worry about Mitch," Knocker said, then stepped away from Jenna and Mitch.

As Mitch watched in total bewilderment, Knocker transformed into a magnificent dragon with blue-green scales and giant, blue wings. He spread his wings wide to show Mitch what he would have been up against should Mitch have challenged him—a very daunting vision indeed. His bright green dragon eyes glared at Mitch as he decreed, "Mitch, you have broken your promise to me, so you must face the consequences. I told you we don't take promises lightly!"

Jenna called out, "Mitch, you should be glad that Knocker is a dragon, otherwise you would suffocate here on the land. He can fly you to the open sea in just a few minutes."

Jenna watched Mitch's face distort as it changed from a human to a shark, forming a large snout with rows of sharp teeth; his eyes slipping to the side of his head as the mouth took on its predator proportions. Once he was completely transformed, Mitch started flailing on the ground, unable to breathe out of water.

Knocker called to Jenna as he flew over to Mitch and picked him up, "Jenna, I will deliver Mitch to the ocean and will be back soon!"

"Thank you, Knocker!" Jenna called as she watched them fly away.

Chapter Eighteen

THE NEXT CHALLENGE

As Knocker flew out of sight, Ituria appeared in the clearing and walked up to Jenna. "Well done, Jenna," he said approvingly, "you have once again saved my friends. We are deeply grateful, thank you."

"You are welcome, Ituria. I am glad I was able to protect Knocker from Mitch. He is my friend too, and it was my honor to protect all my friends here in Middle Forest!" Jenna replied, glad she was able to stop Mitch from finding Knocker.

Turning to speak to the Ike tree, Ituria said, "This place is no longer safe for me because of you!" Anger crept into his voice as he continued. "You and Mitch didn't think about anything but yourselves. Nothing else mattered. But you seek something you can never find—peace. Your whole life you have had to fight, and you killed defenseless animals because it made you feel like you were in control, caring nothing for the animals you slaughtered! And because of you, other hunters will continue coming here, trying to succeed where you, and now Mitch, have failed. However, hunters like you will not win, not as long as there are humans like Jenna!"

A small moaning sound came from the tree as its branches slowly started to droop and several leaves dropped to the ground.

Ituria responded to Ike's plea, "Ike, there is no way to reverse the magic and change you back into the evil human you once were. Furthermore, until you die, you will always be known as the tree that once was Ike, the killer of Ranco. You should hope that someday you will be forgiven by the animals that live here, and you should also hope that careless humans don't decide that you should be cut down to make way for human houses or roads. Farewell, Ike, I shall not see you again."

Ituria turned away from Ike and looked back at Jenna. "Jenna," he said quietly, "let's go meet with your grandfather and update him on the situation. He will be worried. Knocker should be at your house once he has completed his mission."

Jenna nodded and walked toward Ituria, and together they turned to the trail leading to Jenna's home.

"Jenna," Ituria said in a serious tone, "as you know, Celeste and I will no longer be able to visit here in Middle Forest, and Knocker is not safe here either. I have gone to visit the Elders to discuss how we can protect our animal friends here, as they will need a Protector."

"It has been many years since there was any hunting allowed in Middle Forest," Ituria continued, "except for that three-day affair a few months ago after Ike convinced the local government to let him hunt here. The animals who live in Middle Forest are not used to hunters and need someone to protect them against humans."

"Is there anything I can do, Ituria?" Jenna asked sincerely. "You know how much I care for the animals here. They are like my family."

"I have been reviewing all the options, Jenna," Ituria answered. "However, we have never had a human Protector appointed by the Elders before anywhere on Earth. It would take some convincing for them to appoint any human, as their distrust is great."

"I understand," Jenna replied. "What would I need to do to convince them? Is there anything that would make them see how much I care for my friends here? I would do anything to make sure they are safe."

"We discussed several other options in detail, but my mind did keep coming back to you, Jenna." Ituria stopped walking and turned to look at her.

"Jenna," he asked solemnly, "I believe that you would make a worthy Protector. Would you be willing to appear before the Elders to show them you have the courage and spirit needed to protect the animals of Middle Forest?"

Jenna looked at Ituria, thinking of all her friends in the forest and how much they meant to her. "Yes, Ituria," she replied with determination. "Yes, I would do anything to protect my friends, and if I have to prove it to the Elders, I'll be glad to do whatever they ask."

"Thank you, Jenna!" Ituria replied with appreciation. "I know you will be up to anything the Elders require to win their trust!"

"I will do my best, Ituria!" Jenna replied, hoping that she could meet whatever challenges they would put before her. "What do I need to do?"

"Well for now," he responded, "let's get back to your grandfather and Knocker. They will be looking for us at your house. We can discuss further once we get there."

"Sounds good," Jenna said, wanting to let Grandpa know she was okay. A lot had happened since she left him early this morning. She also wanted to make sure Knocker made it back after his trip to drop Mitch off in the ocean.

As they got closer to her house, she could see Grandpa and Knocker in his human form talking in the back yard near the edge of the forest.

"Grandpa," Jenna called out, "we got Dan to leave and made sure Mitch couldn't return to hunt my friends!"

Chapter Nineteen

A NEW PROTECTOR

As Jenna and Ituria approached the edge of the forest that backed up to her yard, Grandpa and Knocker came over to meet them, so that Ituria could remain hidden in the forest.

"Jenna," Grandpa called out as she got closer, "I'm so glad you're safe!"

"I was safe, Grandpa. No need to worry about me," she responded. "Dan has gone back home, and Mitch will never bother you again. We were successful in keeping the hunters out of Middle Forest!"

"Yes, you did a great job! Knocker was telling me about Mitch and how you were able to give him the potion," Grandpa replied proudly.

"Mitch is now swimming in the ocean, Jenna," Knocker added. "You won't have to worry about him ever coming back to Middle Forest!"

"Thank you, Knocker. I appreciate your help in taking him away!" Jenna said, then her tone changed to concern. "However, Knocker, I am worried about others that may come back looking for you. As Ituria said, one hunter tells another, who tells another, all looking for a prize."

"Yes, I understand," Knocker replied with regret. "We will no longer be able to use Middle Forest as our Earth home, and Ituria has been looking for other areas where we will be safe when we have to journey here."

"Russ," Ituria said in a serious voice, "I was talking to Jenna on the way back about needing to assign a Protector to this area. She asked if she could be considered as the new Protector. If we were to take her into consideration, would that be acceptable to you?"

"Jenna," Grandpa said intently as he turned to looked at her, "is this something you want to do? Once you are tested and if you are appointed, you will need to be ready to assist at a moment's notice whenever the wild animals of Middle Forest need you."

"Yes, Grandpa," Jenna replied immediately, her mind already made up. "These animals are my friends, and I will do anything to protect them. I am ready to prove that I can protect them, no matter what the threat!"

Ituria walked over to Jenna and stood in front of her as he said, "Jenna, I did ask the Elders to consider you as the new Protector when I visited them. We do not have any human Protectors, and they were very hesitant. I was able to convince them that your prior actions warranted their consideration, and they agreed to see if you would meet the standards to take on this important role."

"Thank you Ituria, for your faith in me. I appreciate it!" Jenna replied. "Please let me know what tasks they require for me to prove myself to them. I will be glad to undertake any challenge!"

"The Elders agreed to watch how you handled a stressful and dangerous situation, to show that you can handle these situations on your own," Ituria responded, watching Jenna carefully, then waiting for her reaction.

"That is a fair test," Jenna said, nodding to Ituria. "Since you and Knocker will no longer be here. I accept their challenge and will do my best!"

"Jenna, thank you," Ituria responded. "Unknown to you, the Elders have used this latest threat to Middle Forest to observe your courage and spirit. They wanted to see what you would do to protect Middle Forest and its inhabitants, not knowing that you were being watched or evaluated."

"They have been watching you since yesterday when I requested that they consider you," Ituria continued. "They watched as you convinced Dan to leave, and as you confronted Mitch. They also watched as you rescued Sedric, seeing how you respect all the creatures of this forest, and how you were able to use the animals' strengths to help you protect the forest."

"While we were in the forest and you were having Knocker take Mitch to the ocean, they provided me their decision," Ituria said, his voice still serious, "and based on the courage and spirit you showed in your efforts

to protect Knocker, as well as the other animals of Middle Forest, they have agreed to appoint you as the new Protector of Middle Forest. Will you accept this appointment?"

Jenna looked at Ituria for a moment, taking in the announcement. Then she replied with gratitude and respect, "Yes, I do accept! I am honored that they have chosen me. I won't let you down, I promise!"

"Thank you, Jenna," Ituria replied with approval. "I believe you will make a worthy Protector, as you have shown to me and to the Elders you do have the courage and spirit to protect our friends!"

"One other thing that had to be considered though," he continued, "is that as a Protector, you need to be able to communicate with the animals. They have provided me with this necklace, a gift from the Elders, that will allow you to communicate with all animals in Middle Forest at any distance."

Jenna watched as a necklace appeared, floating in the air in front of Ituria. The beautiful light blue variegated stone with the carving of a large bear on the front was attached to a gold chain, sparkling in the sunlight. She reached out and took it, looking at its beauty for a moment before putting it around her neck. "This is so beautiful. I will wear it always!" she exclaimed.

Chapter Twenty

NEW BEGINNING

"Jenna," Ituria declared solemnly, "you are the first human Protector appointed by the Elders. This is not a role to take lightly, as we will depend on you to protect our friends here in Middle Forest. On behalf of the Elders, we thank you for accepting this appointment." Ituria bowed his head to Jenna in recognition of her new role.

Bowing back to Ituria, Jenna responded with respect, "I am glad to receive this important role from the Elders, and I will do my everything in my power to keep Middle Forest safe. Thank you for your trust in me!"

Grandpa walked over and gave Jenna a hug. "I'm proud of you, Jenna! You have shown great courage and I know you will do your best."

"Jenna," Ituria agreed, "you do indeed have great courage. You have also shown that you can control your transformations into a wolf and back to a human. Know that transformations are very much controlled by your emotions, so you must remember to remain calm while in Middle Forest to prevent others from learning of your secret abilities."

"Thank you, Ituria," Jenna responded gratefully. "I will remember!"

"Knocker and I will take our leave of you now, knowing that Middle Forest is in good hands," Ituria said to Grandpa and Jenna. "We will need to get the translation stone back, Jenna; however, you do not need it anymore, as your necklace will allow you to communicate with the animals whenever you want."

Reaching into her pocket, Jenna pulled out the translation stone and handed it to Knocker. "Here you go, Knocker. I wish you well and I hope you find a safe place to visit when you travel to Earth!"

"Thank you, Jenna," Knocker replied as he took the translation stone and put it into his duffle bag. "Thank you for your assistance, and I wish you well in your new role. I have confidence you will be a great Protector!"

"Farewell, Ituria and Knocker," Grandpa called out. "Be safe on your journeys! I look forward to working with you and other members of Ituria's Alliance on your missions to Earth. I am always ready to assist!"

"Thank you, Russ," replied Ituria. "We will reach out to you as needed for future missions. Take care!"

"Farewell, Russ and Jenna. Be safe!" Knocker called as he turned to follow Ituria into the forest.

Jenna and Grandpa watched from the edge of the forest as Knocker transformed back into a dragon. He waved his large blue wings forward and a blue beam of light appeared, heading to the sky. Ituria stepped into the blue beam, and Knocker called out to the sky, "Guardian, we are ready!"

Within seconds, the blue light flashed from the sky, and Knocker and Ituria disappeared. Jenna glanced into the sky in the direction of the light flash and saw that the moon was visible in the sky. *They are back home now!*

Jenna reached for the necklace hanging around her neck, wanting to make sure this was all real, that she really had been appointed to protect her friends in Middle Forest. Holding gently onto the necklace, she looked around the forest, knowing that she was now responsible for all the creatures here. It would be a great challenge, but one she was proud to accept.

"Jenna," Grandpa said, putting his arm around her shoulders as they walked out of the forest, "I am very proud of you. You have proven that you can protect this forest, and I am glad that you have agreed to accept the appointment as Protector!"

"Please feel free to talk with me if you have any questions about protecting the forest," Grandpa continued, "but remember, it will be up to you. Even though I am part of Ituria's Alliance, I am still an old bear, so I won't be able to help you with the protecting part. However, I have the utmost confidence you will be able to handle that on your own, as you have shown today."

"Thank you, Grandpa," Jenna said gratefully. "I know with your guidance we will keep everyone safe here in Middle Forest."

As they walked into the back yard, Grandpa added quietly, "I will work with you to make sure your parents don't find out. The fewer humans who know, the better."

Sedric and Fira ran up to Jenna when she entered the back yard.

"Jenna," Sedric called out excitedly, "we saw Ituria appoint you as our Protector. Thank you for accepting! I'll be glad to help. Just call to me if you need anything!"

"Me, too!" Fira added eagerly.

"Thank you both," Jenna replied with a smile. "I will need everyone's help to protect Middle Forest!"

Ralphie ran over from the porch and joined them, saying, "I'll help too, Jenna!"

As Jenna talked with her forest friends, she was happy that she had been appointed by the Elders to protect them. It was a big responsibility, but one she was glad to accept. She wanted to make sure her friends were safe, and she knew they would all work together to protect Middle Forest!

THE END
—until Jenna's next adventure in Middle Forest!

Note From The Author:

While this may be a fantasy adventure, the story surrounding the gray wolves and many other endangered animals doesn't always have a happy ending.

Recently returned to the list of endangered and threatened species in most of the country by Court Order, the Court protection of gray wolves did not extend to the Northern Rockies. In several states containing the Northern Rockies within their boundaries, state agencies are allowing wolves to be run down by ATVs and snowmobiles, gunned down from helicopters, and even baited out of protected areas like Yellowstone Park just to be killed. One state wildlife agency has even been directed to allow unlimited killings of wolves, killing pups in their dens, and offering a bounty for each wolf killed, encouraging hunters and trappers to go out and wipe out whole packs of wolves for the bounty money.

Gray wolves play a critical role in biodiversity, including culling out weakened elk and deer, keeping the herds strong, and preventing the overgrazing of trees so beavers and riparian birds can also thrive. They are vital to maintaining the health and balance of entire ecosystems. If we do not recognize and protect the roles of all members of the ecosystem, then the entire ecosystem will collapse.

My thanks to the Defenders of Wildlife, Natural Resources Defense Council (NRDC), and many other environmental groups, for taking action to protect the gray wolves and other endangered species.

BOOK CLUB QUESTIONS:

❧⁓❧

1. Who is Marcus?
2. Why was Mitch in Middle Forest a few months prior to his current visit? What were they searching for then? What is Mitch searching for now?
3. Why is Dan so adamant that he will not hunt again?
4. How do Mitch and Dan plan to keep their hunting a secret?
5. Who helps Jenna watch the hunter's camp, letting her know when the first hunter leaves, and where he goes?
6. Who lets Jenna know that Mitch is out laying traps in Middle Forest and is on his way to her house?
7. Why did Ituria decide that he could not use Middle Forest as his Earth base anymore?
8. How did the Elders test Jenna to see if she should be selected as the next Protector?
9. What did Jenna receive from the Elders to allow her to talk to the animals in Middle Forest?
10. Something to think about—what would you do if you were able to talk to the animals?

ABOUT THE AUTHOR

J.B. moved to Florida in her early teens and has lived there ever since, enjoying the mild weather and abundance of wildlife. She even spent several seasons raising orphan squirrels. She graduated from the University of Central Florida and has spent her working career in the legal profession. Her novels are inspired by her family and nature, as well as her need to escape from the real world once in a while.

www.facebook.com/J.B.Moonstar
Instagram@J.B.Moonstar
Twitter@jb_moonstar
Jbmoonstar.author@gmail.com
Website – jbmoonstar.com

Discover more by
JB Moonstar

Chronicles of Ituria

Russ and The Hidden Voice

Taylor and the Red Wolf Rescue

Jenna and the Legend of the White Wolf

Jenna and the Eyes of Fire

Jan and the Secret Cave

Jan and the Search for Lilya

Taylor and the Final Nine

Michelle and the Missing Manatee

Jenna and the Broken Promise

Sara and the Secret Mission

& More Adventures to Come!

The Mermaids of Crystal Cay

Kimmi and the Sea Dragon

Roselia and the Ancient Warriors

& More Adventures to Come!

Coloring Book from
Artist Jenn Kotick

Mermaids

Discover more at
4HorsemenPublications.com

10% off using HORSEMEN10